The Sky Stalker's Prophecy

Mrigendra Bharti

Published by Sellbrochure Vymish Entertainment, 2024.

THE SKY STALKER'S PROPHECY

First edition. July 2, 2024.

ISBN: 979-8224305988

Written by Mrigendra Bharti.

Table of Contents

The Sky Stalker's Prophecy (Preface).. 1

Prologue: 3

About Sellbrochure Vymish Entertainment 5

Introduction: 8

Chapter 1: Introduction and Discovery 10

Chapter 2: Unveiling Secrets 23

Chapter 3: The Long Road Back 39

Chapter 4: Rekindled Light 56

Chapter 5: Whispers in the Dark 70

The Sky Stalker's Prophecy (Preface)

The whispers were faint at first, a mere tremor in the fabric of reality, barely perceptible to all but the most attuned ears. They spoke of a land ravaged by a creeping darkness, a blight that choked the life from the earth and twisted the creatures that dwelled within it. These were the Blighted Lands, a festering wound on the world, a stark reminder of an ancient war against an unseen enemy.

For generations, the whispers remained a chilling folktale, a campfire story whispered amongst trembling villagers. But Alia, a young woman with eyes that mirrored the clear blue sky, felt a deeper connection. The whispers resonated within her soul, a constant hum in the back of her mind, urging her towards a destiny she couldn't yet fathom.

Then, one fateful night, the whispers intensified, morphing into a desperate plea for help. Images of a monstrous entity, the Blight Guardian, rose in Alia's mind – a harbinger of the encroaching darkness. It was a chilling vision, a glimpse into a future that threatened to consume the world.

Driven by an undeniable pull, Alia set out on a perilous journey, guided by the ever-strengthening whispers and the cryptic clues they revealed. A lone rider on a windswept plain, she sought out the Sky Stalker, a mythical creature whispered to be a guardian of the skies, a protector against the unseen threats.

Little did Alia know, her quest would not only test her courage but also uncover an ancient prophecy, one that foretold the rise of a champion wielding a legendary artifact – the Guardian's Shield. This shield, lost to the ages, held the key to sealing the Blighted Lands and banishing the darkness forever.

But the path ahead was fraught with peril. Shadowborn creatures, twisted manifestations of the Blight, lurked in the shadows. Powerful warlords, corrupted by the darkness, sought to exploit the chaos for their own gain. And the Blight Guardian, a monstrous embodiment of pure malice, guarded the source of the corruption with unwavering ferocity.

This is the tale of Alia and her companions, a band of unlikely heroes drawn together by the whispers and united by a common cause. It is a story of courage, sacrifice, and the desperate struggle against a force that threatens to consume everything. This is the story of the Sky Stalker's Prophecy, a prophecy that hinges on a young woman's unwavering determination and the power of an ancient artifact. Let the whispers begin.

Prologue:

The wind howled a mournful song through the skeletal remains of a once-mighty forest. Twisted branches clawed at the blood-red moon, the only light source in this desolate wasteland. The air hung heavy with the stench of decay and a suffocating silence broken only by the wind's mournful cry.

Here, on the fringes of the Blighted Lands, stood an ancient watchtower, its weathered stones etched with forgotten runes. A lone figure, cloaked in a tattered gray robe, stood on the highest platform, their gaze fixed on the pulsating red glow that stained the horizon.

Elder Elara, her weathered face a map of countless years, had spent her life listening. Not to the sounds of the wind or the rustle of leaves, for those were silenced in this blighted land. No, she listened for the whispers - faint echoes carried on the ethereal breeze, remnants of a world ravaged by darkness.

Tonight, the whispers seemed louder, more urgent. They spoke of a shift in the balance, a crack in the barrier that held the Blighted Lands at bay. Images flickered in Elara's mind - monstrous shadows stalking the land, a defiant stand against an overwhelming darkness, a shimmering shield pulsing with an ethereal light.

A shiver ran down her spine. The whispers spoke of a prophecy, a forgotten tale of a champion wielding a legendary artifact. They spoke of a new hope, a flicker of light against encroaching despair.

But hope, like the once-proud trees that littered the Blighted Lands, was a fragile thing. Elara knew the darkness wouldn't relinquish its hold easily. It would fight, twisting and corrupting, seeking to extinguish any spark of defiance.

As the red glow on the horizon intensified, casting an ominous light on her face, Elara tightened her grip on the worn staff in her hand. The whispers grew stronger, clearer, a desperate plea for help. They spoke of a young woman, guided by destiny, who held the key to sealing the darkness away.

Elara closed her eyes, the whispers washing over her. A faint smile touched her lips. The prophecy was awakening. The fight was far from over, but tonight, a flicker of hope had been rekindled in the heart of the Blighted Lands.

About Sellbrochure Vymish Entertainment

Sellbrochure Vymish Entertainment, recognized as India's largest book publishing company, has made significant strides in ensuring its extensive collection of books reaches audiences across the global market. This rapid expansion is a testament to the company's dedication to disseminating knowledge and literature far beyond national borders. Central to its success is its affiliation with InkWhirl Media Networks, a reputable entity in the media and publication industry known for its innovative and strategic approaches. Within this network, InkWhirl Publication LLC operates as a vital division, further enhancing the company's capabilities and reach in the international market.

The visionary behind this enterprise is Mrigendra Bharti, the founder of Sellbrochure Vymish Entertainment. His foresight and passion for the literary world have been instrumental in steering the company towards remarkable growth and recognition. Under his leadership, Sellbrochure Vymish Entertainment has not only expanded its catalog but also established a strong presence in both domestic and international markets. Mrigendra Bharti's commitment to excellence and innovation has been a driving force in the company's journey, ensuring that it stays ahead of industry trends and meets the evolving needs of readers worldwide.

Sellbrochure Vymish Entertainment operates under the robust support of its parental organization, Mrigendra Bharti Group InfoTech. This affiliation provides the necessary resources and strategic guidance, enabling the publishing company to undertake ambitious projects and explore new markets. Mrigendra Bharti Group InfoTech's extensive experience in technology and information services has been a valuable asset, allowing Sellbrochure Vymish Entertainment to integrate advanced digital solutions in its operations, thereby enhancing its distribution capabilities and reader engagement.

Through relentless efforts and a commitment to quality, Sellbrochure Vymish Entertainment continues to break barriers and expand the reach of Indian literature globally. The company's diverse portfolio includes a wide range of genres, catering to different age groups and interests, thereby fostering a rich and inclusive reading culture. As it continues to innovate and grow, Sellbrochure Vymish Entertainment remains dedicated to its mission of making literature accessible to all, contributing significantly to the global literary landscape.

Connect With Mrigendra,
Thank you very much for choosing this book.
You can also connect with me on Instagram,
https://www.instagram.com/i_mrigendrabharti.official
With Love,
Mrigendra Bharti

Introduction:

Alia squinted against the relentless sun, her hand shielding her brow as she scanned the endless horizon. The wind, laden with the scent of sunbaked earth, whipped her hair around her face, carrying a faint, almost imperceptible tremor. It was there and then gone, a fleeting touch on her soul rather than a sound in her ears.

For most, it would be nothing more than a trick of the wind. But for Alia, it was a whisper – a single, fragmented note in a symphony only she could hear. These whispers, a constant hum in the back of her mind, had been her companions for as long as she could remember. They spoke of places she had never been and creatures beyond her wildest imaginings, hinting at a world beyond the sheltered life she knew in the village of Eldoria.

Eldoria, nestled amidst rolling green hills and fertile fields, was a haven of tranquility. But even here, whispers of the Blighted Lands – a desolate wasteland corrupted by an ancient evil – reached them in hushed tones around crackling fires. These were stories of monstrous creatures and a creeping darkness that threatened to engulf the world.

Alia, unlike most villagers who dismissed these tales as mere folklore, felt a strange pull towards them. The whispers resonated deep within her, swirling around her like a persistent, albeit faint, melody. It was a connection she couldn't explain, a yearning for something more, a destiny yet to be unraveled.

One day, the whispers intensified, transforming from a murmur to a desperate plea. Images flooded Alia's mind – a barren landscape, a hulking monstrosity radiating malice, and a shimmering shield pulsing with an otherworldly light. It was a chilling vision, a glimpse into a future that threatened to consume the world.

Driven by an unknown force, a fire ignited within Alia. This was no longer a distant story; it was a call to action. The whispers were not merely tales; they were a plea for help, a message entrusted to her alone.

With a heavy heart, she knew her sheltered life in Eldoria was at an end. The whispers had spoken, and she had no choice but to answer. This was the beginning of her journey, a journey guided by the whispers and fueled by a growing sense of purpose. It was a journey that would redefine her world, test her courage, and pit her against a darkness far older and more terrifying than she could ever imagine. The whispers had led her to the precipice of a grand adventure, and Alia, with a deep breath and a tremor of fear in her heart, was about to step off.

Chapter 1: Introduction and Discovery

Eldoria nestled serenely amidst the towering peaks of the Whispering Mountains. Its quaint houses, built from a warm, honey-colored stone, clung precariously to the slopes like wildflowers defying gravity. The air shimmered with an ethereal glow, the result of an ever-present mist that danced between the mountain crags. This mist, the villagers believed, was the breath of the Whispering Stones, ancient monoliths that dotted the landscape around Eldoria.

Alia, a young girl with eyes the color of moss and hair like spun moonlight, skipped through the cobbled streets, a basket swinging from her arm. Her laughter echoed against the ancient stones, a melody woven into the constant hum of the wind whistling through the mountain passes. At twelve summers old, Alia was as lively and spirited as the mountain streams, her curiosity as boundless as the sky above.

Unlike other children who played tag in the village square or chased butterflies in the meadows, Alia spent her days befriending the Whispering Stones. These colossal sentinels, etched with swirling patterns and forgotten symbols, were more than just landmarks to Alia. They were companions, silent guardians who held ancient wisdom within their weathered surfaces.

One particular morning, Alia approached a towering monolith at the village outskirts. Its surface, rough with age, was cool beneath her touch. She pressed her ear against the stone, a familiar ritual. It was here, in the stillness of dawn, that Alia could hear the faintest whispers emanating from the monolith – whispers that spoke of forgotten stories, of a time when magic pulsed like a heartbeat through the land.

At first, the whispers were unintelligible, a mere murmur against the backdrop of the wind. But with each passing day, Alia honed her ability, learning to decipher the language of the stones. It was a language not of spoken words, but of emotions, of fleeting images, and a deep, resonant hum that resonated within her soul.

Today, as Alia pressed her ear against the stone, the usual gentle whispers were replaced by a tremor, a disquietude that sent shivers down her spine. The images she perceived were fragmented, unsettling – a swirling vortex of darkness devouring a sunlit meadow, a chilling wind howling through abandoned houses. Fear tingled at the edges of her consciousness, a foreign sensation in the haven of Eldoria.

Alia pulled back from the stone, a frown creasing her brow. It wasn't just this particular monolith; all the Whispering Stones were emitting the same unsettling tremors, their whispers laced with a sense of foreboding. She hurried back to the village, her heart pounding a frantic rhythm against her ribs.

Back in the bustling village square, Alia found the villagers gathered. Faces etched with concern, they huddled around a central well, the usually crystal-clear water now swirling with an unnatural murkiness. The elder, a wizened figure with eyes the color of the twilight sky, stood at the well's edge, his brow furrowed in concentration.

Alia pushed through the crowd, urgency propelling her forward. "What's wrong, Elder Elara?" she asked, her voice breathless.

"Something troubles the heart of the mountains, young one," Elara replied, his voice raspy with age. "The whispers of the stones have grown dark, filled with shadows."

A chill ran down Alia's spine. The elder, the village's conduit to the stones, echoed her own disquiet. The fear she'd felt earlier now solidified, a cold stone settling in her stomach.

Elder Elara extended a frail hand towards Alia. "Come, child. We must listen to what the stones have to say."

Together, they walked towards the outskirts of Eldoria, the elder leaning heavily on Alia's shoulder. The village square, once filled with laughter and chatter, now lay shrouded in a veil of apprehension. The tremors in the air were more pronounced now, a low rumble that resonated in Alia's very bones.

As they neared the Whispering Stones, Alia felt a surge of energy emanating from the monoliths, a pulsating darkness that clawed at the edges of her consciousness. She squeezed her eyes shut, trying to decipher the chaotic whispers.

Images flashed before her inner eye: a monstrous entity with eyes of burning embers, its touch withering everything it touched. Fear morphed into a fierce determination. She had to understand, had to help.

Pushing through the growing darkness, Alia focused on the whispers, her senses straining to make sense of the fragmented messages. Slowly, the whispers coalesced, forming a chilling prophecy. It spoke of a creeping darkness, a force that would shroud the mountains in shadow, consume the light within Eldoria, and extinguish the whispers of the stones forever.

Alia stumbled back, gasping for breath. Her face, pale as moonlight, reflected the growing dread that gripped her heart. The playful spirit of a moment ago had vanished, replaced by a solemn understanding of the looming threat.

Elder Elara, sensing her distress, placed a comforting hand on her shoulder. "The stones speak of darkness, young one, but they also whisper of hope. There is one who can stand against this shadow, one who can listen to the stones and understand their message."

Alia stared at the elder, his words resonating within her. The whispers had been fragmented, but a single image flickered repeatedly – a young woman, her eyes glowing with an ethereal light, her hands reaching out to silence the tremors in the earth.

"Who is she?" Alia's voice trembled, a whisper mirroring the tremors of the stones.

"The chosen one," Elder Elara replied, his gaze meeting hers. "The one who can hear the whispers."

A shiver ran down Alia's spine. The image from the whispers, the hope it offered, mirrored her own unique gift. But could a young girl like her, barely on the cusp of womanhood, truly be the village's savior?

The elder saw the doubt reflected in her eyes. "Alia," he said, his voice firm yet gentle, "the stones have spoken. Their whispers may be cryptic, but they are seldom wrong. You have a special connection to them, young one. A connection that could be the key to our survival."

Alia looked at the Whispering Stones, their immense forms silhouetted against the darkening sky. The tremors had subsided, replaced by an ominous stillness. Yet, she could still feel a faint pulse within the earth, a low hum that resonated with a growing sense of urgency within her.

Suddenly, a chilling wind swept down from the mountains, carrying with it the scent of decay and something... unnatural. The villagers, who had been observing their conversation from a distance, let out a collective gasp.

Alia turned towards them, their worried faces reflecting the fear now blooming in her own heart. The darkness was closer than she'd imagined, its chilling presence a palpable force in the air.

"We need to warn the villagers," she said, her voice surprisingly steady. "Tell them to prepare for what's coming."

Elder Elara nodded, his face etched with worry. "Yes, child. But there is more. We need to understand what this darkness is, where it comes from. Only then can we hope to fight it."

Alia understood. The whispers had been fragmented, offering a glimpse of the danger but not its source. If they were to have any chance of stopping this darkness, they needed to learn more.

"I'll go back to the stones," Alia offered, determination returning to her voice. "I'll try to decipher more from their whispers."

Elder Elara's face softened with gratitude. "Be careful, child. This darkness... it seems malevolent."

Alia gave him a reassuring nod, though fear still gnawed at her insides. This darkness, whatever it was, felt ancient and powerful. But she would not give in to fear. She was the one who could understand the stones, the one who could hear their whispers. And that, in this moment, was the village's only hope.

Turning back towards the Whispering Stones, Alia felt a surge of courage. She took a deep breath, the crisp mountain air filling her lungs. The task ahead was daunting, but she wouldn't face it alone. The villagers, united by the common enemy, stood behind her. And the stones, with their ancient wisdom, would be her guide.

As dusk settled over Eldoria, casting long shadows across the land, Alia approached the monoliths with renewed determination. The whispers were waiting, a tapestry of emotions and fragmented images yearning to be unraveled. Tonight, Alia would listen, and she would understand.

With renewed resolve, Alia stood before the Whispering Stone, its surface cool and rough against her palm. The wind howled around her, carrying the chilling scent of the encroaching darkness. Taking a deep breath, she closed her eyes, shutting out the world and focusing entirely on the stone.

This time, the whispers were different. The initial tremor was absent, replaced by a deep, melancholic hum that resonated deep within her soul. Images flickered in her mind's eye, fragmented and fleeting. A lush valley, once vibrant with life, now shrouded in an unnatural darkness. Plants withered and died, their vibrant hues replaced by a sickly gray. Eerie, guttural growls echoed in the distance, a sound devoid of life or warmth.

Alia pushed further, straining to understand the whispers. Slowly, the fragmented images coalesced into a story, a tragic tale of a forgotten past. She saw a powerful artifact, a crystal pulsating with an ethereal light, hidden within a forgotten temple deep within the mountains. This artifact, the whispers conveyed, was a source of immense power, capable of nurturing life or plunging the world into darkness.

But something had gone wrong. The artifact had been corrupted, its once life-giving energy twisted into a malevolent force. The whispers hinted at a betrayal, a power-hungry individual who sought to control the artifact for their own gain. This corruption, the whispers revealed, was the source of the encroaching darkness.

Alia recoiled, a sob escaping her lips. The darkness wasn't a natural force, but a consequence of greed and ambition. The weight of this knowledge settled heavily upon her. The fate of Eldoria, and perhaps beyond, rested upon her ability to decipher this ancient story and find a way to uncorrupt the artifact.

Opening her eyes, Alia surveyed the darkening landscape. The villagers huddled within their homes, their faces etched with worry. Elder Elara stood a few paces away, his eyes filled with concern.

"Alia," he said softly as she approached, "what have the stones revealed?"

Alia took a deep breath, her voice trembling slightly. "It's an artifact, Elder. A powerful one that has been corrupted."

She relayed the story she gleaned from the whispers, the vibrant valley succumbing to darkness, the betrayal that twisted the artifact's power. As she spoke, a sense of dread settled over the villagers, a collective understanding of the magnitude of the threat they faced.

"Do the stones offer any solution?" Elara asked, his voice laced with desperation.

Alia closed her eyes, focusing once again on the faint hum of the stone. It was a long shot, but she had to try. "There might be," she said, opening her eyes. "The whispers hint at a way to cleanse the artifact, to restore its balance. But it's... difficult. It requires someone with a deep connection to the stones."

Elder Elara's eyes widened. He looked at Alia, the unspoken truth hanging heavy in the air. The burden of responsibility, heavy and daunting, settled on Alia's shoulders. She, a young girl on the cusp of womanhood, was the bridge between the villagers and the ancient wisdom of the stones. She was the one who held the key to saving Eldoria from the encroaching darkness.

"But I'm still learning," Alia stammered, the weight of the task threatening to overwhelm her. "I don't know if I can do it alone."

A comforting hand closed over hers. She looked up to see Elder Elara gazing at her with a resolute expression. "You are not alone, child," he said gently. "We are all in this together. The villagers, myself... we will help you in any way we can."

A spark of hope ignited within Alia. She wasn't alone. She had the villagers, their unwavering support, and the wisdom of the elder guiding her. And most importantly, she had her unique connection to the Whispering Stones.

Taking a deep breath, Alia straightened her shoulders. Fear was still present, a niggling voice at the back of her mind. But along with it came a newfound determination. She wouldn't let the darkness consume Eldoria. She would decipher the whispers, find the solution, and cleanse the corrupted artifact.

"There's no time to waste," Alia declared, her voice ringing with newfound resolve. "We need to find a way to reach the temple and cleanse the artifact before it's too late."

Elder Elara nodded, his weathered face etched with grim determination. "Then we begin our preparations at dawn," he said. "Together, we shall face the darkness."

The villagers, emboldened by Alia's newfound confidence, emerged from their homes. A sense of unity and purpose filled the air, a silent promise to face the coming darkness together.

As the first rays of dawn painted the sky with streaks of gold and rose, the villagers of Eldoria gathered in the village square. A somber mood hung heavy in the air, a stark contrast to the usual morning bustle. Yet, beneath the worry, a flicker of determination burned in their eyes.

Alia stood at the forefront, her slight frame shrouded in a worn cloak. The weight of responsibility pressed heavily upon her, but her heart hammered with a newfound resolve. She had spent the night deciphering the whispers further, gleaning fragmented details about the forgotten temple.

Elder Elara stood beside her, his presence a source of strength and wisdom. He raised his hand for silence, and the villagers fell quiet.

"The whispers have spoken," he began, his voice raspy but firm. "They have revealed the source of the darkness and a potential path to salvation."

He explained the legend of the artifact and its corruption, his words painting a vivid picture of the devastation it could wreak. A collective gasp rippled through the crowd.

Alia stepped forward, her gaze meeting the villagers' anxious eyes. "The whispers also speak of a way to cleanse the artifact," she said, her voice gaining confidence with each word. "But it is a perilous journey, fraught with dangers."

She described the treacherous path to the forgotten temple, guarded by ancient traps and monstrous creatures born of the darkness. The villagers listened intently, their faces grim, but a resolute determination glimmered in their eyes.

"We cannot stand idly by while our home is threatened," declared a burly blacksmith, his voice booming across the square. "We stand with you, Alia! Together, we will face whatever dangers lie ahead."

A ripple of agreement surged through the crowd. Alia felt a warmth spread through her chest – a surge of gratitude for the unwavering support of her village. She wasn't alone in this fight.

"We need to prepare," Elder Elara interjected. "The whispers speak of ancient weapons and protective charms hidden within the village." The next few hours were a flurry of activity. Villagers, young and old, gathered supplies and unearthed forgotten relics – enchanted blades forged by ancestors, shields imbued with the mountain's strength, and potions brewed with ancient herbs.

Alia, guided by the whispers and Elder Elara's knowledge, helped select the most potent tools for their quest. She felt a sense of connection to the artifacts, a tingling warmth that flowed through her fingertips as she touched the enchanted weapons.

Finally, as the sun climbed its peak, a small group of volunteers stepped forward. There was the stalwart blacksmith, his face set with grim determination. A nimble young hunter, her eyes sharp and her movements as fluid as the mountain streams. And a wizened herbalist, her weathered hands clutching a satchel brimming with potions.

These were the bravest of the villagers, those willing to risk their lives to save their home. Alia looked into their faces, each etched with concern but unwavering resolve. She saw not just fear, but a deep love for Eldoria and a fierce loyalty to their community.

"We may be few," Alia addressed them, her voice steady, "but we are united. And the whispers of the stones guide us."

Elder Elara placed a hand on Alia's shoulder. "May the mountains watch over you, child," he said, his voice thick with emotion. "Remember, the whispers are your compass. Trust their guidance."

Alia nodded, a fierce determination burning in her eyes. She took a deep breath, the weight of responsibility settling on her shoulders. Today, they ventured into the heart of darkness, a small band of villagers on a mission to save their home.

With a final farewell, they set out from the village, walking towards the first whisper on the wind, the first step on a perilous journey into the unknown. The path ahead was shrouded in darkness, but so too was it laced with a faint glimmer of hope – the hope that the whispers would lead them to salvation, and that Alia, the young girl who could hear the stones, would be their guide.

Chapter 2: Unveiling Secrets

Days bled into weeks as Alia and her companions traversed the treacherous mountains following the cryptic whispers of the stones. The initial exhilaration of their mission had morphed into a steely resolve. The once idyllic landscape had transformed into a menacing terrain, the familiar peaks now shrouded in an unnatural mist that choked the air and obscured the path ahead.

Alia, ever attuned to the whispers of the stones, felt an oppressive silence gnawing at her. The once vibrant hum that resonated from the monoliths back in Eldoria had become faint, a mere echo lost in the swirling darkness.

"Do you think we're on the right path?" Elara, the elder, asked, his weathered face etched with worry as he trudged through the ankle-deep mud. "The whispers have grown scarce."

Alia stopped, her brow furrowed in concentration. She pressed her ear against a moss-covered boulder, hoping to catch a whisper, any whisper, that could guide them. The silence stretched, punctuated only by the howling wind and the creaking of ancient trees burdened by an unnatural weight.

Disappointment gnawed at her. Had they strayed from the path? Was the darkness actively suppressing the whispers, cutting them off from their guide? She closed her eyes, focusing her entire being on the faintest tremor in the earth, the slightest vibration in the air.

Then, a flicker – a faint hum, barely perceptible against the howling wind. Alia's eyes snapped open, a flicker of hope igniting within her. The whispers were weak, but they were there.

"They're faint," she said, her voice barely a whisper itself. "But they're still there. This way."

Pointing in the direction of the faint hum, Alia led the group deeper into the wilderness. The terrain grew even more treacherous, the path choked with thorny vines and fallen trees. The air grew colder, biting into their exposed skin, and the unnatural mist swirled around them, obscuring their vision.

Suddenly, a guttural growl echoed through the trees, sending shivers down their spines. A monstrous creature, its body a grotesque amalgamation of shadow and bone, lurched out from the mist. Its eyes, burning embers in the gloom, locked onto Alia, the only member of the group whose face remained uncovered.

A surge of adrenaline coursed through Alia's veins. The whispers had warned of these creatures, born from the darkness and driven by an insatiable hunger.

"It's a Shadowhunter!" Elara shouted, his voice laced with fear. "We need to fight it off!"

The blacksmith, ever the warrior, stepped forward, his axe gleaming in the dim light. The hunter, nimble and quick, drew her bow, an arrow nocked and aimed at the creature's heart. Alia, however, felt a strange pull towards the Shadowhunter. It was more than just fear; it was a sense of recognition, a faint echo of the creature's darkness.

As the creature lunged, a guttural roar escaping its throat, Alia instinctively did something she had never done before. She reached out with her mind, focusing on the faint whisper within the darkness that resonated with her own connection to the stones.

A wave of confusion washed over the Shadowhunter, its feral rage momentarily disrupted. It blinked its fiery eyes, momentarily disoriented. Using this brief window of opportunity, the blacksmith swung his axe with a mighty roar, the blade cleaving through the creature's shadowy form. It let out a shriek that tore through the air before dissolving into wisps of darkness that dissipated into the swirling mist.

Alia slumped against a nearby tree, her breath coming in ragged gasps. The mental exertion had drained her, leaving her feeling lightheaded and exhausted. The others stared at her, stunned silence hanging heavy in the air.

"Alia," Elara spoke finally, his voice filled with awe. "You..."

"I felt it," Alia said, her voice shaky but filled with wonder. "I felt the darkness within it, just like I hear the whispers of the stones."

The revelation hung heavy in the air, a new and unexpected turn of events in their quest. Alia, with her unique connection to both the stones and the darkness they were fighting, might hold the key to navigating this treacherous journey and unraveling the secrets of the corrupted artifact.

But the triumph was short-lived. The faint hum of the whispers grew stronger, but it was laced with a sense of urgency, a warning of a greater danger looming ahead. With renewed determination and a newfound understanding of her own abilities, Alia led the group deeper into the heart of the darkness, following the whispers towards the forgotten temple and the secrets it held.

The whispers grew stronger, leading Alia and her companions towards a towering wall of sheer rock that seemed to cleave the mountain itself. The air grew thick with a strange energy, making their hair stand on end and their skin prickle. The unnatural mist swirled around them, clinging to their clothes and obscuring their vision.

"The whispers say there should be an entrance here," Alia said, her voice barely audible over the howling wind. "But I see nothing."

Elara squinted at the rock face, his hand running over the moss-covered surface. "There might be a hidden mechanism," he muttered, his voice laced with frustration.

The blacksmith, ever practical, slammed his fist against the rock wall. "Let's just break it down then!"

Alia held up a hand, her fingers outstretched towards the rock wall. "Wait," she said, focusing on the pulsating hum of the whispers. "There's something... a pattern."

Closing her eyes, Alia delved deeper into the whispers, tracing the faint vibrations resonating within the rock. Images flickered in her mind's eye – swirling patterns, ancient symbols etched onto the stone. She opened her eyes, a jolt of understanding shooting through her.

"There are symbols!" she exclaimed, pointing to specific spots on the rock wall. "They match the whispers. We need to activate them in a specific order."

With renewed purpose, the group worked together. Elara, with his knowledge of ancient languages, deciphered the meaning of the symbols. The blacksmith, using his strength and tools, carved them more clearly onto the surface. The hunter, nimble and agile, climbed higher to reach markings out of their reach.

Alia, meanwhile, felt the whispers come alive as they deciphered the symbols. The rock face pulsed with a faint light, responding to their actions. Following the sequence dictated by the whispers, they activated the symbols one by one.

A low rumble echoed through the mountains as the final symbol flared with light. The wall of rock split open, revealing a hidden passage shrouded in perpetual darkness. An icy wind, heavy with the scent of time and forgotten secrets, blew from the opening.

"This is it," Alia whispered, a shiver running down her spine. "The whispers lead here."

The group, their faces etched with a mixture of trepidation and determination, exchanged a look. Taking a deep breath, they stepped into the darkness, the entrance sealing shut behind them with a thunderous clang. They were left in an inky blackness, the silence broken only by the rasping of their own breaths.

Emerging from their packs, they lit torches, their flickering flames casting dancing shadows on the walls. The passage sloped down, leading them deeper into the heart of the mountain. As they walked, the whispers grew louder, filled with a sense of awe and forgotten grandeur.

Suddenly, the passage opened into a vast cavern flooded with an ethereal light. Suspended in the center of the cavern, bathed in a soft luminescence, floated a network of intricate structures carved from a strange, translucent material.

Buildings, walkways, and bridges formed a miniature city, silent and desolate.

"It's... beautiful," Alia breathed, captivated by the sight.

"A hidden city," Elara murmured, his voice filled with wonder. "Lost to the ages."

As they ventured further into the cavern, the whispers grew stronger, revealing the city's history. It was a civilization that had thrived in harmony with the mountains, harnessing the power of the Whispering Stones for peace and prosperity.

But the whispers also spoke of a betrayal, a lust for power that led to the corruption of the artifact and the subsequent downfall of the city. This, they realized, was the source of the darkness that threatened Eldoria.

Their exploration led them to the heart of the city, a towering structure that pulsed with a faint, sinister energy. It was the temple, the final resting place of the corrupted artifact. The whispers, now laced with urgency, warned them of the dangers that lay within.

Standing before the temple doors, a sense of foreboding settled over the group. They had reached their destination, but the true challenge was just beginning. They had to confront the darkness within the temple, cleanse the artifact, and restore balance before it consumed Eldoria.

Taking a deep breath, Alia reached out towards the massive stone doors of the temple. The whispers intensified, a cacophony of emotions swirling within her. This was it. The fate of Eldoria rested on their shoulders. With a determined glint in her eyes, Alia pushed open the doors, the heavy stone groaning in protest.

The darkness within the temple gaped at them, a hungry maw promising oblivion. Unfazed, Alia and her companions stepped into the unknown.

The temple entrance slammed shut behind them with a resounding boom, plunging them into an inky blackness. The only light came from their flickering torches, casting grotesque shadows that danced on the damp stone walls. The air hung heavy with a stale, oppressive silence, broken only by the ragged gasps of Alia's companions as they struggled to adapt to the sudden darkness.

Alia, ever attuned to the whispers, felt a shift in the direction of their guidance. No longer was there a single, clear hum leading them forward. Instead, the whispers became a cacophony of fragmented emotions – fear, despair, and an underlying current of malevolent power.

"Stay close," she whispered, her voice barely a tremor in the stifling silence. "The whispers warn of dangers unseen."

They proceeded slowly, their senses on high alert. The cavern floor was slick with moisture, each step a treacherous gamble on uneven ground. The air grew colder, the temperature dropping with every step deeper into the temple's heart.

Suddenly, a low growl echoed from the darkness ahead. Their torches illuminated a pair of glowing red eyes embedded in a hulking shadowy form. Panic surged through the group as the creature, another Shadowhunter but larger and more grotesque than the one they encountered before, lunged at them.

The hunter reacted instinctively, loosing an arrow that struck the creature in the shoulder. It roared in pain, but the wound seemed to have little effect. The blacksmith charged forward, swinging his axe with a mighty yell. The blade connected with the creature's leg, severing it clean.

But before their victory cry could escape their lips, another Shadowhunter emerged from the darkness, and then another. They swarmed the group, their monstrous forms fueled by the corrupting darkness within the temple.

Alia, overwhelmed by the sheer number of creatures, closed her eyes and reached out with her mind. This time, the whispers were a raging torrent of fear and fury emanating from the Shadowhunters themselves. But amidst the chaos, she sensed a flicker of something else – a faint echo of their former selves, a glimmer of a memory before their corruption.

Focusing on this flicker, Alia projected a calming wave of energy towards the creatures. The effect was instantaneous. The Shadowhunters faltered, their movements sluggish, their eyes momentarily filled with confusion. This brief window of opportunity was all they needed.

With renewed vigor, the group fought back, their weapons flashing in the dim light. The blacksmith, fueled by adrenaline, cleaved through the Shadowhunters with his axe. The hunter, nimble and agile, danced around their attacks, her arrows finding their targets with deadly accuracy.

Alia, channeling the whispers' guidance, targeted specific pressure points on the creatures, temporarily disrupting their corrupted minds. One by one, the Shadowhunters fell, dissolving into wisps of darkness that dissipated into the cavern air.

Gasping for breath, the group leaned against the damp stone walls, their bodies trembling from the exertion. They had survived, but the encounter had taken its toll.

"There are too many of them," the hunter panted, her voice laced with fear. "We can't fight our way through this."

Elara nodded grimly. "We need a strategy. The whispers might hold the key."

Alia closed her eyes, focusing on the echoes of the whispers in her mind. The fragmented emotions lingered, but beneath it all, she sensed a faint path, a hidden passage leading deeper into the temple.

"There's another way," she said, her voice filled with newfound determination. "The whispers show a hidden corridor behind a false wall. It leads to the inner sanctum."

With newfound hope, the group surveyed the cavern. Following the whispers' guidance, they searched for any inconsistencies in the stonework. Finally, after several agonizing minutes, they found a section of the wall that felt slightly looser than the rest. The blacksmith, using his strength and tools, pried open the stones, revealing a narrow passage shrouded in darkness.

"This is it," Alia whispered, stepping forward. "The whispers lead here."

The group, exhausted but resolute, entered the hidden passage. The darkness seemed to press down on them, thick and suffocating. They huddled together, their torches casting faint beams that barely penetrated the gloom. The whispers grew stronger, but now they held a tinge of warning, urging them to be silent, to move with stealth.

As they ventured deeper, the whispers revealed a horrifying truth. The corrupted artifact wasn't just contained within the temple; it was the temple itself. The ancient structure, once a beacon of power and harmony with the Whispering Stones, had been twisted by the darkness, its very essence now warped by the corrupting influence.

The passage led them to a large chamber, its ceiling lost in the darkness. In the center of the vast chamber, bathed in an eerie green glow emanating from the ceiling, stood the corrupted artifact. It resembled a giant crystal, its once perfect clarity now fractured and swirling with a sickly, pulsating light. The whispers screamed in Alia's mind – a cacophony of pain, rage, and a terrifying sense of hunger.

As they approached the artifact, Alia felt its power tug at her very being, a darkness seductive and alluring. Memories flickered through her mind – visions of power beyond comprehension, of bending the very fabric of reality to her will.

But the whispers also conveyed a sense of betrayal, of a civilization consumed by their own greed. Alia recoiled, the seductive whispers replaced by a surge of determination. She wouldn't succumb to the darkness' allure.

"It feeds on negativity," Elara rasped, his voice tight with fear. "We need to stay focused, clear our minds of darkness."

Following his advice, Alia closed her eyes, focusing on the faint hum of the whispers that resonated with the purest aspect of the stones – a calm, unwavering energy. Slowly, she felt the darkness recede, replaced by a sense of serenity.

Opening her eyes, she looked at the artifact. "The whispers say it can be cleansed," she announced, her voice steady. "But it requires pure energy, a connection to the true essence of the stones."

Elara stepped forward, his face creased with worry. "You, child. You have that connection."

Alia nodded, a knot of fear tightening in her stomach. She knew the risk. Channeling such a vast amount of energy could leave her drained, vulnerable.

The herbalist approached her, handing her a vial filled with a shimmering liquid. "This," she said, her voice raspy but firm, "will enhance your connection to the stones and amplify your energy. But use it sparingly, child. It is potent."

Taking a deep breath, Alia uncorked the vial and swallowed its contents. A rush of warmth flooded her body, and the connection to the Whispering Stones intensified a hundredfold. The whispers became clear, a chorus of voices guiding her towards the artifact.

With trembling hands, Alia extended them towards the pulsating crystal. The energy crackled in the air, arcing between her fingertips and the artifact's surface. The corrupted light within the crystal writhed in protest, a maelstrom of darkness battling the pure energy emanating from Alia.

The group watched in awe and trepidation as Alia, a young girl on the cusp of womanhood, stood defiant against the corrupting power of the artifact. Her body tensed, sweat beading on her brow as she poured her entire being into the cleansing ritual.

The chamber trembled, the air thick with crackling energy. The whispers reached a crescendo, a frantic plea from the ancient stones to break free from the darkness. Then, with a final burst of blinding light, a wave of pure energy surged from Alia, engulfing the corrupted artifact.

For a moment, there was an agonizing silence. Then, a transformation began. The sickly green glow within the artifact dimmed, replaced by a soft, ethereal light that pulsed in harmony with the whispers. The fractures in the crystal mended, its surface becoming flawless once more.

Alia slumped to her knees, drained of energy. The herbalist rushed to her side, administering a potion to revitalize her. The others, faces etched with relief, watched in awe as the cleansed artifact bathed the chamber in a soft, welcoming light.

The darkness, severed from its source, began to recede. The whispers, now free from the corruption, resonated with a profound sense of peace and gratitude. Alia felt a warmth bloom within her, a connection to the stones stronger than ever before.

But their victory was bittersweet. The temple remained corrupted, a husk of its former glory. The whispers, however, hinted at a way to heal the temple, to restore it to its original state. This, however, would have to wait.

For now, their primary mission was complete. The darkness had been defeated, its source cleansed. As the light from the artifact cast long shadows across the cavern floor, Alia knew their journey was far from over. They had to return to Eldoria, share the news of their success, and begin the process of healing the land.

But for tonight, they allowed themselves a moment of respite, basking in the aftermath of their victory. They had ventured into the heart of darkness and emerged triumphant, their bond forged by courage and a shared purpose. As they stood together, bathed in the soft glow of the cleansed artifact, Alia knew that they had not only saved Eldoria but also rekindled the whispers, ensuring a future where the village and the Whispering Stones lived Their moment of triumph was short-lived. A tremor shook the chamber, sending dust raining down from the ceiling. The once serene whispers turned frantic, a chorus of warnings echoing in Alia's mind.

"Danger!" she gasped, scrambling to her feet. "The whispers warn of a collapse!"

Elara assessed the situation with a practiced eye. "We need to get out of here, now!"

Panic surged through the group as they scrambled towards the hidden passage. The tremors intensified, chunks of stone crumbling from the ceiling. The once smooth passage was now a treacherous obstacle course, littered with debris and precariously balanced boulders.

Alia, fuelled by adrenaline and the whispers' guidance, led the way. The herbalist, weakened from her earlier potion, stumbled and fell. The blacksmith, ever the protector, scooped her up, his powerful arms carrying them both through the collapsing tunnel.

The hunter, swift and agile, navigated the treacherous path with practiced ease. Elara, his face etched with worry, brought up the rear, ensuring no one was left behind.

Behind them, the tremors grew more violent. The air was thick with dust and the deafening roar of crumbling stone. The whispers, filled with urgency, pleaded for them to hurry.

Finally, after an eternity of scrambling and dodging falling debris, they emerged from the hidden passage. Relief flooded them as they stood panting in the main temple chamber. But their reprieve was short-lived.

The cavern rumbled, a deep groan echoing through the mountains. Cracks snaked across the ceiling, growing wider with each passing second. The whispers, now tinged with despair, revealed the horrifying truth – the temple was collapsing.

"We have to go!" Elara roared, his voice raw with urgency.

Without hesitation, the group turned and bolted out of the temple doors. They burst out into the cavern, the once-hidden city of the ancients exposed to the cold mountain air. But they didn't stop. Their only thought was to get as far away from the collapsing temple as possible.

Behind them, the ground trembled. With a deafening roar, the temple imploded upon itself, a massive cloud of dust engulfing the cavern. The once majestic city of the ancients was swallowed whole, leaving behind a gaping chasm in the mountainside.

As the dust settled, Alia and her companions stood on the edge of the crater, their faces streaked with soot and sweat, their bodies trembling with exhaustion. They had escaped, but their hearts ached for the loss of the ancient city, a silent testament to a civilization lost to darkness.

Looking around them, Alia realized they were far from familiar territory. The path they had taken through the hidden passage had led them deeper into the mountain, far from the entrance they had found before.

They were lost. But amidst the desolation, a sliver of hope remained. The whispers, though faint now, still resonated in Alia's mind – a beacon guiding them back to Eldoria, back to their village, back to the warmth of home.

With a deep breath, Alia squared her shoulders, her resolve hardening. They may be lost, but they were not broken. Their journey wasn't over. They would find their way back, carrying within them the knowledge of their victory and the hope for a future free from darkness.

Taking the lead once more, following the fading whispers in her mind, Alia began to walk. The setting sun cast long shadows across the treacherous mountain landscape, but Alia and her companions pressed forward, united by their shared purpose and guided by the faint echoes of the Whispering Stones.

Chapter 3: The Long Road Back

Days blurred into weeks as Alia and her companions trudged through the unforgiving mountain terrain. The thrill of their victory at the temple had long since dissipated, replaced by the constant gnawing of hunger, the ever-present threat of exposure, and the nagging worry of being hopelessly lost.

Alia, once filled with a boundless energy fueled by her connection to the Whispering Stones, felt her reserves dwindling. The whispers, once a clear and constant hum in her mind, now echoed faintly, their guidance flickering like a dying candle in the wind.

The group, their initial bravado worn thin by the harsh conditions, fell into a somber routine. The blacksmith, ever the stoic leader in Elara's absence, shouldered the burden of hunting for food and setting traps. The hunter, nimble and resourceful, scouted ahead, searching for safe passage and signs of civilization. The herbalist, her once vibrant spirit dimmed by illness, focused on using her remaining strength to tend to their wounds and ailments.

Elara, burdened by his role as the elder, was a shadow of his former self. His face, etched with worry lines, reflected the despair creeping into their hearts. He constantly scanned the horizon, searching for any landmark that might point them towards Eldoria.

One particularly bleak evening, as they huddled around a meager fire, the silence punctuated only by the crackling flames and the howling wind, Elara spoke, his voice raspy with fatigue.

"Alia," he said, his eyes filled with a profound sadness, "the whispers... they are fading."

Alia's heart sank. She knew he was right. The faint guidance that had led them through the treacherous mountains was growing fainter with each passing day. Fear, cold and sharp, clawed at her stomach. Without the whispers, they were truly lost, adrift in a vast wilderness with no hope of finding their way back.

"Don't give up, Elara," she forced a smile, her voice more reassuring than she felt. "The whispers may be faint, but they are still there. We can rely on them, and... and we have each other."

The others offered weak smiles in response, but the forced cheer did little to dispel the growing gloom. As the fire died down, casting long shadows across their weary faces, a heavy silence descended upon the group.

Sleep, when it finally came, was troubled by nightmares. Alia dreamt of Eldoria, the once peaceful village shrouded in an unnatural darkness. She saw the villagers, their faces etched with despair, pleading for her help. She woke from her restless sleep with a gasp, sweat clinging to her body, the fear from the dream lingering in the pit of her stomach.

The following morning, as they set out to resume their journey, Alia felt a strange sensation – a tug within her, a faint echo of the familiar hum of the whispers. At first, she dismissed it as a trick of the mind, a desperate yearning for their former guidance. But the sensation persisted, growing stronger with each passing step.

Following this faint pull within her, Alia led them on a path that diverged from their usual course. The landscape became steeper, the climb more arduous. The hunter voiced her concern, but Alia, driven by the newfound pull, pressed on.

After a grueling climb, they reached a ridge overlooking a vast valley. As they crested the ridge, a gasp escaped Alia's lips. Spread out before them, nestled amidst the rolling hills, lay a village unlike any they had seen before.

The architecture was unlike the familiar wooden structures of Eldoria. Buildings of a polished, white stone shimmered in the morning sunlight, radiating an aura of peace and serenity. Smoke curled from chimneys, and fields of vibrant green stretched towards the horizon. A winding river, like a silver ribbon, snaked through the valley, adding to the idyllic scene.

Alia felt a surge of hope, a tremor of excitement course through her. Could this be a sign? Had the whispers, faint as they were, guided them to a place of refuge?

Elara, his face etched with a mixture of caution and curiosity, approached Alia. "Do the whispers... do they guide us towards this place?"

Alia shook her head, her brow furrowed in concentration. "They're... different. Weaker, but... welcoming."

The decision to descend into the valley was a difficult one. They were weary, cautious of strangers, and unsure if they would be welcomed. But the lure of warmth, food, and the hope of potential information about their location proved too strong to resist.

With a shared look of determination, they began their descent into the valley. As they drew closer to the village, they noticed figures moving about, tending to the fields or going about their daily routines. These people were unlike any they had encountered before. Their clothes were made of a fine ...woven fabric, adorned with intricate patterns in vibrant colors. Their faces, though weathered from life in the mountains, held a warmth and openness that put Alia and her companions at ease.

As they approached the village gate, a tall, elderly man with a long, flowing beard stepped forward. His eyes, a clear blue that reflected the summer sky, held a kind curiosity.

"Welcome, travelers," he greeted them, his voice deep and gentle. "We haven't seen strangers around these parts in a long time. What brings you to the Hidden Valley?"

Alia, ever the spokesperson, bowed respectfully. "We are travelers from Eldoria," she explained, her voice hesitant. "We have been lost in the mountains for many weeks. The whispers of the stones... they led us here."

The elder's eyes widened in surprise. "Eldoria? But that village lies far to the south. How did you find yourselves lost so far north?"

Alia recounted their arduous journey, omitting details about the corrupted artifact and the collapsing temple. The elder listened intently, his expression growing solemn as she spoke.

"The whispers..." he murmured, stroking his beard thoughtfully. "They rarely guide strangers this far north. You must have a strong connection to them for them to lead you here."

A glimmer of hope flickered in Alia's chest. "Do you know of Eldoria?" she asked eagerly. "Have you heard anything about the village?"

The elder's face remained unreadable. "There have been... rumors," he said slowly. "Of a darkness that has descended upon the village, whispers of corrupted energy emanating from the Whispering Stones."

Alia's blood ran cold. The elder's words confirmed her worst fears. The darkness she had encountered at the temple was not contained within the mountains; it had somehow reached Eldoria.

"They need help," she whispered, her voice trembling. "We have to get back."

The elder's gaze softened. "That may be difficult, child. The journey back south is long and treacherous, even for those who know the way. But..." he paused, a hint of a smile playing on his lips, "the whispers are strong with you. Perhaps they can guide you home once more."

He gestured towards the village. "Stay with us in the Hidden Valley for a while. Rest, replenish your supplies, learn more about the whispers. There is much you don't know."

Alia glanced at her companions, their faces etched with fatigue but a spark of hope lighting their eyes. Accepting the elder's offer was a risk, a delay in their journey back to Eldoria. Yet, the promise of knowledge and a chance to strengthen her connection to the whispers was too enticing to ignore.

With a nod of agreement, Alia turned to her companions. "We will stay," she announced. "For now."

The following weeks in the Hidden Valley were a revelation for Alia and her companions. The villagers, led by the elder they came to know as Kael, were skilled hunters, farmers, and weavers. They lived in harmony with nature, relying on the guidance of the Whispering Stones for their way of life.

Unlike the villagers of Eldoria who passively relied on the stones to provide for their needs, the people of the Hidden Valley actively learned to understand the whispers. Kael, a master of this art, became Alia's mentor. He taught her how to focus her mind, how to distinguish between the whispers' fragmented emotions, and how to interpret their subtle nuances.

Alia's connection to the stones deepened with each passing day. Under Kael's tutelage, she learned to channel their energy, not just for healing, but also for communication. She began to understand the whispers as a language, a complex code of emotions, sensations, and images.

The rest of the group also benefited from their stay. The blacksmith learned new forging techniques from the villagers' skilled metalworkers. The hunter, through observation and practice, honed her tracking skills and learned to navigate by the stars. The herbalist, under the care of the village healer, began to recover her strength and knowledge, learning new medicinal uses for the plants that grew abundantly in the valley.

But the knowledge that Eldoria was in peril cast a shadow over their peaceful existence. Every day, Alia felt the pull to return, to face the darkness that threatened her village. Every night, she dreamt of her family and friends, their faces etched with worry and fear.

One clear night, as Alia sat on a hill overlooking the valley, bathed in the silvery light of the full moon, she reached out with her mind, focusing on the faint whispers from the south. The connection was weak, distorted by distance and the mountains, but she persevered.

Images flickered through her mind's eye – dark tendrils spreading from the Whispering Stones in Eldoria, choking the life out of the land, villagers

...weakening under the strain of the corrupted energy. A surge of fear threatened to overwhelm Alia, but she clung to the whispers, drawing strength from the faint connection.

Suddenly, a new image flashed in her mind – a figure shrouded in darkness, standing at the heart of the village, seemingly directing the spread of corruption. The figure emanated a malevolent power, its form shifting and swirling, defying definition. A jolt of recognition shot through Alia. It was the Shadow King, the embodiment of darkness they had encountered at the temple in a weakened state.

A chilling realization settled in Alia's stomach. The corrupted artifact had not been the source of the darkness; it was merely a conduit. The true source, the Shadow King, had somehow escaped his imprisonment and reached Eldoria, directly corrupting the Whispering Stones there.

Now, understanding tinged the urgency that had gnawed at her for weeks. This wasn't just about cleansing the temple artifact; it was about confronting the Shadow King himself and severing his connection to the Whispering Stones.

Returning to the village, Alia found Kael by the fire, his weathered face lit by the flickering flames. "We can't stay here any longer," she declared, her voice filled with newfound resolve.

Kael, his gaze steady, seemed to have anticipated her decision. "I know, child," he said gently. "The whispers have spoken. Eldoria needs you."

Alia felt a wave of gratitude wash over her. Kael, ever wise and perceptive, understood the urgency of their mission.

"But you cannot face this darkness alone," he continued. "The whispers guide many paths, not just yours. There is another who may be able to aid you."

Kael led Alia to a secluded part of the village, away from the watchful eyes of the villagers. There, in a hidden clearing bathed in the ethereal light of luminous plants, stood an old woman, her wrinkled face etched with wisdom and a faint luminescence emanating from her eyes.

"This is Elara," Kael explained, his voice reverent. "She is the last of the Whisperers, a lineage who once wielded the power of the stones for the greater good."

Elara's gaze locked with Alia's, a knowing glint in her eyes. "The whispers have spoken of you, child," she said, her voice raspy but firm. "You are the bridge, the one who can understand both the whispers and the power within the stones."

A flicker of hope ignited within Alia. With Elara's knowledge and her own connection to the whispers, perhaps they could stand a chance against the Shadow King's darkness.

Elara explained that the lineage of Whisperers had dwindled over the years, their powers waning as villagers grew complacent, relying solely on the stones' passive sustenance. However, Elara still possessed a vast knowledge of the stones' true potential, and with a little training, she could help Alia unlock her own abilities.

The next few days were a whirlwind of focused training. Elara, drawing upon the whispers and her own fading power, taught Alia how to channel the energy of the stones into offensive techniques – protective shields, bolts of pure energy, and the ability to sense the presence of the Shadow King's corruption.

The training was grueling, pushing Alia to her physical and mental limits. But fueled by the desire to save Eldoria and the unwavering support of her companions, she persevered.

Finally, the day arrived when they felt ready. With heavy hearts, they bade farewell to the villagers of the Hidden Valley, their gratitude etched deep within them. Kael, ever the wise leader, provided them with supplies, maps, and words of encouragement.

Standing at the edge of the valley, Alia took a deep breath, channeling the whispers to guide their way. The path ahead was long and fraught with danger, but they were no longer lost travelers. Now, they were a band of heroes, armed with knowledge, courage, and the power of the whispers, ready to face the darkness that threatened their home.

With determination in their eyes, they set off, leaving behind the peaceful sanctuary of the Hidden Valley and venturing forth into the treacherous mountains once more.

This time, their journey had a renewed purpose – to confront the Shadow King, cleanse the Whispering Stones of Eldoria, and restore light to their beloved village. They were the bridge between the whispers and the stones, and they were the only hope for Eldoria's future.

Their journey back to Eldoria was arduous. The whispers, though stronger with Elara's guidance, remained distorted by distance. The mountains, once a vast unknown, now seemed even more menacing as they navigated treacherous slopes and unforgiving terrain.

Days bled into weeks. Hunger gnawed at their bellies, and fatigue weighed heavily on their limbs. The blacksmith's strength, once boundless, began to wane. The hunter, ever agile, found her movements less sure-footed. The herbalist, though her health had improved significantly, still grappled with lingering weakness.

Alia, fueled by a burning determination, remained resolute. She spent every waking moment honing her newfound abilities, channeling the whispers' energy to create shimmering shields for protection and focusing her mind to sense the ever-growing tendrils of darkness emanating from Eldoria.

One particularly bleak evening, as they huddled around a meager fire amidst a howling snowstorm, Elara spoke, her voice laced with concern.

"The darkness is growing stronger," she warned, her eyes reflecting the dancing flames. "I can feel its tendrils stretching further, reaching out to consume more land."

A pang of fear gripped Alia. They were closer to Eldoria than they had been in weeks, yet the urgency to reach their destination had become overwhelming. The whispers, once a steady hum, were now a frantic plea, urging them to hurry.

"We can't afford to rest," Alia declared, her voice firm despite the tremor in her heart. "We need to push on, even through the night."

The others, their faces etched with weariness, looked at each other in silent agreement. They understood the gravity of the situation. Eldoria, their home, their families, were in peril. Sleep, a luxury they craved, would have to wait.

Under the cloak of a starless night, they continued their journey, guided only by Elara's knowledge of the terrain and the faint whispers resonating in Alia's mind. The biting wind whipped at their faces, the snow crunching under their boots the only sound in the vast silence.

As dawn approached, casting a faint light upon the horizon, they reached a ridge overlooking a familiar landscape. A gasp escaped Alia's lips. There, nestled in the valley below, lay Eldoria – but it was no longer the peaceful village she remembered.

A shroud of darkness seemed to cling to the land. The once vibrant fields were now barren and lifeless. Houses, once bustling with life, stood silent, their windows like empty sockets. The Whispering Stones, once a beacon of light and harmony, now glowed with an unnatural, sickly green luminescence, pulsating with malevolent energy.

Alia felt a surge of despair, a cold dread that threatened to consume her. But amidst the bleakness, she saw a flicker of hope. Smoke curled from a single chimney in the center of the village – a sign that some villagers still held on, waiting for a miracle.

"We have to get there," Elara rasped, her voice filled with a mixture of grief and determination.

Alia nodded, a fierce resolve hardening her resolve. This was it. The culmination of their long journey, their training, their sacrifice. They were here to face the darkness, to cleanse the stones, and to save Eldoria.

With renewed strength, they descended the ridge, their steps lighter despite the weight of their mission. As they approached the village, an unsettling silence fell over them. The whispers in Alia's mind screamed with a sense of dread, pinpointing the source of the darkness – a tall, ominous structure that had been erected in the village square, its obsidian walls pulsating with an evil energy.

This was the heart of the corruption, the nexus through which the Shadow King channeled his power. They had to reach it, to destroy it, and sever his connection to the Whispering Stones.

Suddenly, figures emerged from the shadows, their eyes vacant, their faces twisted into grotesque masks. They were villagers, once friendly neighbors, now corrupted puppets of the Shadow King. With a guttural roar, they charged towards the group.

A battle ensued, a desperate fight for survival. The blacksmith, his axe flashing in the morning light, held off a flurry of attacks. The hunter, her arrows finding their mark, brought down corrupted villagers before they could reach them. The herbalist, drawing upon her remaining strength, used her knowledge of plants to create makeshift weapons and concoctions to deter the attackers.

Alia, channeling the whispers' energy, formed a shimmering shield around the group, deflecting blows and pushing back the corrupted villagers. But with every passing moment, the darkness seemed to grow stronger, its tendrils reaching out to ensnare them.

Elara, her face etched with strain, raised her hand. With a cry that seemed to shatter the silence, she unleashed a wave of pure ...energy, a blinding white light that ripped through the corrupted villagers, forcing them back with screams of pain. The darkness recoiled for a moment, the unnatural glow from the obsidian structure flickering momentarily.

Elara, however, stumbled back, her face pale, her hand trembling. The effort had drained her significantly.

"We have to reach the structure!" Alia cried, her voice hoarse. "That's the source of the darkness!"

Understanding dawned on the others' faces. The blacksmith, ever the protector, cleared a path with his axe, while the hunter provided cover with her arrows. Alia, drawing on the whispers and the last dregs of her own energy, propelled a powerful energy blast at the corrupted villagers, momentarily forcing them back.

They ran through the gauntlet, dodging and weaving through the corrupted villagers, their lungs burning, their legs threatening to give way. Finally, they reached the base of the obsidian structure. It loomed over them, a malevolent monolith radiating an oppressive aura.

Alia searched for a way in, her eyes scanning the smooth, black surface. The whispers, frantic and distorted, offered no guidance. Despair threatened to engulf her, but then, she noticed a faint inscription above a barely discernible crack in the structure. It was a symbol, an ancient language only vaguely familiar to Elara.

"The language of the Whisperers," Elara rasped, her voice weak but firm. "It's a key."

With renewed hope, Alia focused on the inscription, channeling the whispers. Images flooded her mind – a sequence of movements, a specific combination of touches on the symbol. It was a test, a challenge set by the ancient Whisperers to protect the stones' true power.

With trembling hands, Alia mimicked the movements in her mind. The crack in the structure widened, a sliver of light spilling out. Alia, taking a deep breath, plunged into the unknown, the others close behind.

They found themselves in a dark chamber, the air thick with a suffocating darkness. The malevolent energy pressed down on them, threatening to crush their spirits. In the center of the chamber stood a swirling vortex of black energy – the heart of the darkness, the conduit through which the Shadow King controlled the corrupted stones.

And there, before the vortex, stood the Shadow King himself. He was a towering figure, his form a shifting mass of shadows, his eyes burning with malevolent red light. His voice, a raspy whisper that echoed in their minds, filled the chamber.

"Foolish mortals," he hissed. "You dare challenge my power? You are but insects crawling against a hurricane."

Alia stepped forward, her voice surprisingly steady. "We are here to cleanse the stones, to banish your darkness from our land."

The Shadow King laughed, a chilling sound that scraped against their very souls. "You cannot defeat me. I am the embodiment of darkness, the inevitable end. This world will crumble under my power, and the stones will fuel my rise!"

He raised his hand, channeling a wave of dark energy towards them. Alia, drawing upon the whispers and the last vestiges of her strength, erected a shimmering shield, barely holding back the onslaught.

Elara, despite her weakened state, joined the fight. With a renewed burst of energy, she unleashed another wave of pure light, momentarily disrupting the Shadow King's concentration.

This was their chance. Alia, fueled by the whispers' guidance and a desperate hope, focused her mind on the vortex's dark energy. She visualized the corrupted stones, the suffering they inflicted upon Eldoria. Then, with a surge of power that surprised even her, she slammed her fist outwards, not at the Shadow King, but at the vortex itself.

A blinding light erupted from Alia's hand, engulfing the vortex. The Shadow King shrieked in fury, his form writhing in pain. The corrupted energy recoiled, retreating back into the vortex. The once vibrant black tendrils turned a sickly gray, dissipating into nothingness.

The chamber trembled, the obsidian structure groaning in protest. The unnatural glow from the structure above them flickered and died, revealing the familiar sky through a now-open ceiling.

The Shadow King, weakened and enraged, lashed out, his tendrils of darkness reaching for them. But they were too late. The vortex, its connection to the stones severed, imploded in on itself, dragging the Shadow King with it. A scream ripped through the chamber, echoing with a chilling finality.

Silence descended upon the chamber, broken only by the ragged gasps of Alia and her companions. They had done it. They had defeated the Shadow King, cleansed the stones, and saved Eldoria.

Exhaustion washed over Alia, her legs buckling beneath her. The others, no better, collapsed beside her. But amidst the overwhelming fatigue, a wave of relief and joy washed over them. They had faced the darkness and emerged victorious.

Chapter 4: Rekindled Light

A weak, golden sunlight streamed through the gaping hole in the ceiling of the obsidian chamber, illuminating the dust motes dancing in the air. Alia lay sprawled on the cold floor, her muscles screaming in protest. Every fiber of her being ached, her head pounding like a drum. Yet, a sense of overwhelming relief and exhilaration coursed through her. They had done it. They had defeated the Shadow King and cleansed the Whispering Stones.

Slowly, her gaze swept around the chamber. The once malevolent vortex was gone, replaced by an empty void. The obsidian structure, its power source severed, stood inert, a chilling monument to their victory.

A cough brought her attention to Elara, who lay a few feet away, her face pale but a triumphant glint in her eyes. The herbalist and the blacksmith, though visibly shaken, were also regaining their strength. A wave of gratitude washed over Alia. They had faced this darkness together, and together, they had overcome it.

"We... we did it," Elara rasped, her voice hoarse but filled with emotion.

Alia nodded, a weak smile gracing her lips. "We did."

The moment of victory, however, was short-lived. The gravity of their situation settled back upon them. Eldoria, the village they had fought so desperately to save, lay shrouded in a thick silence. The darkness, though banished from the stones, still lingered over the land, a chilling reminder of the ordeal they had endured.

Alia pushed herself to her feet, her movements stiff and sore. With a hand outstretched, she helped Elara stand. The others, following suit, brushed off the dust and grime of battle, their faces etched with a mixture of exhaustion and determination.

"We have to get back to the village," Alia announced, her voice firm despite the tremor in her soul. "We don't know how badly they've been affected."

The group made their way out of the chamber, the acrid scent of burnt stone clinging to the air. As they emerged into the village square, a gasp escaped Alia's lips. The destruction was worse than she ever could have imagined.

Houses lay in ruins, their roofs collapsed under the weight of a thick, black sludge that had seeped from the corrupted stones. The once vibrant fields were barren, the life choked out by the darkness. The air hung heavy with a deathly silence, a stark contrast to the cheerful bustle Alia remembered.

They wandered through the deserted streets, calling out for any sign of life. Their voices echoed eerily in the emptiness, met only by the mournful creak of swaying branches.

Suddenly, a whimper broke the silence. Following the sound, they found a small figure huddled beneath the twisted wreckage of a house. It was a young boy, no older than ten, his face streaked with tears and fear.

Relief flooded through Alia. Here, at least, was one survivor.

In broken sobs, the boy recounted the horrors they had endured. The creeping darkness, the voices in their heads, the villagers who had fallen victim to the corruption, turning violent and unpredictable. He had only managed to survive by hiding, remaining silent and unseen.

The raw emotion in the boy's voice brought a lump to Alia's throat. This was the price they had paid for their victory, the devastation wrought by the darkness. A wave of doubt threatened to engulf her. Could Eldoria ever recover from such a blow?

Elara knelt before the boy, her voice gentle and calming. "Don't worry, young one," she reassured him. "We're here now. The darkness is gone. We will rebuild our village."

The boy looked at her with wide, hopeful eyes. Alia saw a flicker of the same spirit that had fueled their fight – the unwavering hope for a brighter future.

Alia knelt beside Elara. "We need to find the others," she said, her voice filled with renewed purpose. "They must be scared and in need of help."

Together, they explored the village, searching every corner for any sign of survivors. Their task was arduous, filled with the heartbreak of witnessing the destruction. But they also found pockets of hope – a hidden cellar where a family had taken refuge, a grandfather shielding his grandchildren from the darkness.

By nightfall, they had managed to gather a small group of survivors – a dozen in total, their faces etched with fear and exhaustion. The once vibrant Eldoria seemed eerily small now, its population decimated by the darkness.

As they huddled around a makeshift fire in the remnants of the village square, Elara addressed the survivors, her voice cracking with emotion. She spoke of the Shadow King's defeat, the cleansing of the stones, and their hope for the future.

A fragile glimmer of hope flickered in the eyes of the villagers. They clung ..to Elara's words like a lifeline, a desperate desire for normalcy after the horrors they had witnessed. With the fire crackling and casting flickering shadows on their faces, Alia scanned the group, her heart heavy with a new responsibility.

"We are all that remains," she said, her voice surprisingly steady. "But we are not alone. We have each other. And we have the Whispering Stones."

A murmur of uncertainty rippled through the group. The once benevolent stones had been the source of their suffering, a stark reminder of the darkness they had faced.

Alia understood their hesitation. But she also knew that the Whispering Stones were not inherently evil; they were simply a powerful tool, susceptible to corruption. With the Shadow King vanquished, they could be used again for good, to help them rebuild their lives.

"The whispers have spoken," Elara said, her voice gaining strength. "The stones are no longer corrupted. They are ready to heal the land, to provide us with what we need."

Alia focused her mind, channeling the whispers. Images flickered in her vision – lush fields teeming with life, houses rebuilt and bustling with activity. This was their future, a future they could create with the help of the Whispering Stones.

Reaching out with her mind, she connected with the stones, hesitant at first. The whispers, once distorted and chaotic, were now clear and calming. They pulsed with a gentle energy, a promise of renewal.

A sense of relief washed over Alia. The connection was broken, but the message was clear. The stones were no longer a threat; they were their key to recovery.

Taking a deep breath, Alia addressed the survivors once more. "The whispers confirm it," she declared. "The stones are no longer corrupted. They offer us their power to heal the land, to rebuild our lives."

Her words sparked a hesitant hope in the villagers' eyes. The blacksmith, a man of logic and action, spoke first. "Can these whispers be trusted? How do we know they won't turn against us again?"

Alia understood his skepticism. "The whispers were corrupted before," she admitted. "But the Shadow King is gone. Now, they are a beacon of hope, a guide for us to move forward."

Elara stepped forward, her gaze unwavering. "We can learn to understand the whispers better. We can learn to harness their power responsibly. Together, we can rebuild Eldoria, stronger than ever before."

A murmur of agreement began to spread through the group. The survivors, weary but resilient, yearned for a sense of normalcy. The whispers, once a symbol of fear, now seemed like a potential lifeline.

With a newfound sense of purpose, the group set about planning their next steps. The herbalist, her knowledge of local plants bolstered by her experience with the village elder in the Hidden Valley, identified herbs that could help restore the barren soil. The blacksmith, ever the leader, began organizing plans for rebuilding their homes. Under Elara's careful guidance, Alia honed her ability to channel the whispers, learning to distinguish subtle variations in their energy.

The process of rebuilding was arduous. The Whispering Stones, though no longer corrupted, needed to be realigned, their power directed towards healing the land. Days turned into weeks, weeks into months. Slowly, a faint green tinge began to appear on the once barren fields. Walls were rebuilt, homes restored, and the faint hum of life returned to the village.

The whispers, once a distant echo in Alia's mind, became a constant companion. She learned to translate their fragmented emotions into instructions, guiding the villagers in their efforts. The whispers spoke of patience, of resilience, of the interconnectedness of all living things.

One crisp autumn morning, Alia stood on a hill overlooking the village. The once barren fields were now a patchwork of green, dotted with families tending their crops. Laughter echoed in the air, a sound that had been absent for far too long. The once vibrant Eldoria was slowly coming back to life.

Eldoria had been scarred by the darkness, its population decimated, its innocence lost. Yet, amidst the ruins, a new spirit bloomed – a spirit of resilience, of hope, and of a deep connection to the land. Now, the villagers didn't just rely on the whispers; they understood them, utilizing their power responsibly to nurture their land and build a stronger community.

A smile tugged at Alia's lips. This was a victory far greater than simply defeating the Shadow King. It was a victory of the human spirit, a testament to the power of hope and the enduring connection with the natural world. And as long as they listened to the whispers, as long as they worked together, Eldoria would not only survive, it would thrive. But their journey wasn't over. The whispers spoke of other threats...looming on the horizon, faint but persistent. Threats that required not just their newfound understanding of the whispers, but also a willingness to venture beyond the familiar boundaries of Eldoria.

Alia shared these concerns with Elara, their faces etched with worry beneath the warm glow of the fire that crackled in the rebuilt village square. "The whispers speak of shadows lurking in the far north," Alia explained, "forces of chaos that threaten to disrupt the natural balance."

Elara, her eyes filled with wisdom gathered over a lifetime, nodded slowly. "The whispers have always guided us toward harmony with our surroundings," she said. "If these shadows threaten that balance, we cannot ignore them."

A disquiet settled over the group of survivors gathered around the fire. The memory of the Shadow King's reign was still fresh, a constant reminder of the dangers that lurked beyond their peaceful village.

The blacksmith, ever the pragmatist, voiced the group's apprehension. "We've barely rebuilt our lives here," he said. "Are we strong enough to face another threat already?"

Alia understood his concern. Yet, the whispers were insistent. The shadows in the north, if left unchecked, could eventually engulf Eldoria and disrupt the delicate balance of the land. Ignoring them wasn't an option.

"We don't have to face this alone," Elara interjected. "The whispers also speak of others, scattered across the land, who share our connection with nature. Perhaps by finding them, we can build a network of guardians, a force strong enough to face any threat."

A flicker of hope ignited in Alia's eyes. If others existed with a similar connection to the whispers, their combined knowledge and abilities could be formidable. This wasn't just about protecting Eldoria; it was about safeguarding the natural world itself.

"Then we must find them," Alia declared, her voice ringing with newfound determination. "We can learn from each other, share our experiences, and together, ensure the whispers continue to guide us towards a brighter future."

The villagers, though hesitant, were swayed by Alia and Elara's conviction. They had seen firsthand the devastating consequences of neglecting the whispers. And the idea of a larger community, a united force for good, held a powerful allure.

Their journey north would be fraught with danger, venturing into the unknown. But the whispers were their guide, and their newfound understanding, their strength. They would carry with them the lessons learned from their encounter with the Shadow King - the importance of unity, resilience, and the unwavering connection to the natural world.

Alia, the bridge between the whispers and the villagers, emerged as their leader. Elara, with her vast knowledge and calming presence, became their advisor. The blacksmith, along with skilled hunters and scouts, formed the backbone of their defense. Together, they prepared for their journey, gathering supplies, honing their skills, and strengthening their connection with the whispers.

As the first rays of dawn painted the sky a fiery orange, Alia stood at the head of a small group assembled on the outskirts of the village. They were not warriors, but protectors, carrying with them the hope of Eldoria and the responsibility to preserve the balance whispered by the land itself.

With a deep breath, Alia focused her mind, channeling the whispers. Images flickered in her vision – a towering mountain range shrouded in mist, a hidden valley pulsing with vibrant life. It was the north, their destination, a place where the whispers spoke of others who shared their connection.

With a resolute nod to Elara and a glance back at the newly rebuilt Eldoria, a symbol of their resilience, Alia turned and led her companions northward. The journey was a test of their strength and their newfound understanding. They encountered treacherous landscapes, hostile creatures, and remnants of the Shadow King's influence. But with each challenge, their bond grew stronger, their determination unwavering.

The whispers, their constant companion, guided them through treacherous paths, warned them of approaching dangers, and offered glimpses of the communities they sought.

Weeks turned into months, the landscape growing ever more rugged and unforgiving. But finally, one day, as the sun dipped below the horizon, casting long shadows across the land, Alia felt a shift in the whispers. They pulsated with a newfound intensity, a sense of anticipation.

"We're close," she announced, her voice hoarse with exertion but filled with excitement.

Following the whispers' lead, they emerged into a hidden valley bathed in an ethereal glow. Lush vegetation carpeted the ground, vibrant flowers bloomed in profusion, and crystal-clear streams snaked through the verdant landscape. In the distance, nestled amongst the trees, smoke curled from a cluster of thatched-roof houses.

Alia's heart pounded with a mixture of nervousness and anticipation. They had found them - a community living in harmony with nature ...guided by whispers similar to their own. It was a moment of profound vindication, a confirmation of the whispers' guidance and the potential for a larger network of guardians.

As they approached the village, a group of figures emerged, their faces etched with curiosity but devoid of hostility. They were clad in simple garments of woven natural fibers, their skin tanned by the sun and wind. A sense of peace and harmony radiated from them, a stark contrast to the weary travelers.

Alia, stepping forward with Elara by her side, addressed them with a mixture of nervousness and hope. "We come in peace," she declared, her voice echoing in the quiet valley. "We are from Eldoria, guided by the whispers."

A woman, her face lined with wisdom and adorned with intricate tattoos that seemed to mimic natural patterns, stepped forward. "Welcome, travelers," she said, her voice warm and welcoming. "The whispers have spoken of your arrival. We are the Keepers of the Grove, a community dedicated to living in harmony with nature."

Relief washed over Alia. These were not enemies, but kindred spirits. She explained their journey, their battle against the Shadow King, and their quest to find others who shared their connection with the whispers.

The Keepers listened intently, their faces etched with concern at the tale of the Shadow King. They confirmed the whispers' warnings about the growing shadows in the north, a threat they too had felt stirring within the land.

A week passed as Alia and Elara shared their experiences with the Keepers, exchanging knowledge and techniques for using the whispers. The Keepers, in turn, introduced them to their peaceful way of life, their deep understanding of the natural world.

One evening, as they sat around a crackling fire under a canopy of stars, the elder of the Keepers spoke in a grave voice. "The whispers speak of a darkness that grows stronger," she said. "It threatens to engulf not just our lands, but the very essence of nature's balance."

Alia felt a shiver crawl down her spine. The whispers had revealed dangers, but this sense of urgency was new. "What can we do?" she asked, her voice firm despite the rising fear in her heart.

The elder smiled sadly. "The whispers offer a path, but it is one fraught with danger. They speak of a hidden artifact, deep within the corrupted lands, that holds the key to sealing the darkness away. It is a task that may require sacrifice, but it is the only hope for restoring balance."

Alia and Elara exchanged a glance. The journey north had been arduous, but this new quest was even more daunting. Yet, they knew they couldn't turn back. The whispers had chosen them, and the fate of the natural world rested on their shoulders.

"We will help," Alia declared, her voice resolute. "We faced the Shadow King and emerged victorious. We can face this challenge too."

The elder nodded, a flicker of hope igniting in her eyes. "Then let us prepare you. The whispers will guide you, but the path will be treacherous. You will need not only your newfound understanding, but also courage, resilience, and the unwavering support of your companions."

Alia looked at Elara, the blacksmith, and the other villagers who had accompanied her. They were weary, but their faces were set with determination. Together, they had faced darkness and emerged stronger. Now, they were more than just villagers; they were a band of guardians, united by their connection to the whispers and their unwavering commitment to protecting the natural world.

With the support of the Keepers, they honed their skills, learned the secrets of navigating corrupted lands, and prepared for the perilous journey ahead. They knew that the fate of their world, and the whispers that guided them, hung in the balance.

As dawn broke, casting a golden hue over the peaceful valley, Alia stood at the head of her companions. They exchanged farewells with the Keepers, a silent promise etched in their eyes. It was a time of quiet determination, a somber acceptance of the risks they were about to face.

Turning away from the sanctuary of the Grove, Alia focused her mind, channeling the whispers. Images flickered in her vision – a desolate landscape shrouded in darkness, a pulsating core of malevolent energy. It was the heart of the corrupted lands, their destination, and the potential key to sealing away the encroaching darkness.

With a deep breath and a resolute nod to her companions, Alia led them forward, venturing into the unknown. The journey ahead would be fraught with danger, but they were no longer scared. They were the guardians, chosen by the whispers, and they were determined to protect the light.

Chapter 5: Whispers in the Dark

The wind howled like a banshee across the desolate plains, whipping sand into a frenzy that stung exposed skin and blurred vision. Alia squinted through the swirling dust, her cloak billowing around her like a tattered flag. Days had bled into weeks since they had left the serene haven of the Keeper's Grove, and the once verdant landscape had been replaced by a barren wasteland.

They were on the cusp of the Blighted Lands, a region corrupted by the Shadow King's influence. The whispers grew fainter here, their once clear instructions turning into a distorted hum. The very air vibrated with a malevolent energy, a chilling reminder of the darkness they were about to face.

Alia scanned the group behind her. Elara, despite the toll the journey had taken, exuded a quiet strength. The blacksmith, ever the pragmatist, gripped his axe tightly, his eyes narrowed against the swirling sand. The other villagers, their faces etched with weariness but their resolve unwavering, followed close behind.

They had faced challenges before - treacherous landscapes, hostile creatures, and remnants of the Shadow King's corruption. But this felt different. The Blighted Lands were an embodiment of pure evil, a place where the whispers themselves seemed to struggle to penetrate the thick veil of darkness.

"How much further?" Elara rasped, her voice barely audible over the howling wind.

Alia focused her mind, channeling the distorted whispers. Images flickered in her vision – a desolate mountain range, a single jagged peak piercing the obsidian sky. At its base, a pulsating red glow emanated from a fissure in the rock – the heart of the corruption, the location of the artifact they sought.

"There," she said, pointing towards the distant mountains. "The whispers say it's within those peaks, hidden deep within the corrupted land."

A murmur of apprehension passed through the group. The Blighted Lands were a place of legends, whispered stories of terrifying creatures and irreversible curses. The closer they ventured, the more Alia felt a sense of unease gnawing at her. This wasn't just the harsh environment; it was something deeper, a malevolent presence that seemed to seep into her very bones.

As dusk approached, casting long, ominous shadows across the already bleak landscape, they reached the foothills of the desolate mountains. The wind seemed to die down, replaced by an eerie silence that pressed down on them like a suffocating blanket. The whispers, once distorted, were now completely absent, as if the very air itself refused to carry their message.

Alia halted, a prickling sensation crawling up her spine. "The whispers are gone," she announced, her voice echoing in the unnatural silence.

Elara stepped forward, her brow furrowed in worry. "What does that mean?"

Alia shook her head, uncertainty swirling in her gut. "I don't know. But we can't turn back now. We've come too far."

With a heavy heart, she led the group forward, relying on her sense of direction and the faint trail left by an ancient path long buried in the shifting sands. The barren mountains loomed ahead, their jagged peaks scraping the twilight sky. As they ventured deeper, the air grew colder, the darkness thicker.

Suddenly, a guttural shriek pierced the silence, tearing through the oppressive stillness. Alia whirled around, her hand instinctively flying to the hilt of the dagger strapped to her thigh. The darkness seemed to writhe, shadowy figures emerging from the depths of the valley. They were humanoid in form, but their skin was a sickly gray, their eyes glowing with malevolent red light.

These were the denizens of the Blighted Lands, creatures twisted by the Shadow King's corruption. Alia recognized them from stories whispered around crackling fires in Eldoria – the Shadowborn.

Before Alia could issue a warning, the Shadowborn charged, their guttural roars echoing through the valley. The villagers, their hearts pounding, drew their weapons – swords, axes, and crude spears. A fierce battle ensued.

Alia danced through the fray, channeling what little understanding of the whispers remained. She used the flickering shadows to her advantage, moving faster than the lumbering Shadowborn. Her dagger, imbued with Elara's ancient enchantments, flashed through the darkness, finding gaps in the creatures' defenses.

Elara, despite her age, fought with surprising agility, her staff blurring as she parried and struck with practiced ease. The blacksmith, a force of nature with his mighty axe, cleaved his way through the horde, his booming battle cries rallying the group.

The other villagers fought with a desperation born of their experiences. They had seen what darkness could do, and they were determined to stop it at all costs. But the Shadowborn seemed endless, their claws tearing, their teeth gnashing.

Just as exhaustion began to overwhelm them, a blinding light erupted from the sky, momentarily driving back the darkness. A colossal creature, its wings outstretched blotting out the stars, swooped down upon the battlefield. Its feathers, the color of polished obsidian, shimmered with an otherworldly luminescence. Its eyes, burning with an ethereal blue fire, scanned the scene with chilling intensity.

A gasp escaped Alia's lips. It was a Sky Stalker, a mythical creature of immense power, rarely seen outside of ancient legends. But what was it doing here, in the heart of the Blighted Lands?

As quickly as it appeared, the Sky Stalker focused on the Shadowborn, its screech echoing through the valley like the tolling of a death knell. With razor-sharp talons and a blinding beak, it tore through the horde, its attacks swift and merciless.

The tide of the battle turned. The Shadowborn, seemingly startled by this unexpected attacker, faltered for a moment. The villagers, seizing the opportunity, pressed their advantage with renewed vigor. With the Sky Stalker leading the charge, they pushed back the creatures, driving them deeper into the darkness.

The battle raged for what seemed like an eternity, the air thick with the scent of blood and burning flesh. Finally, with a last, desperate roar, the remaining Shadowborn retreated into the shadows, vanishing as quickly as they had appeared.

Exhausted and battered, the group stood panting in the aftermath of the fight. The Sky Stalker, having dispatched the last of the Shadowborn, landed gracefully on a nearby rock. Its gaze, still alight with its unearthly blue fire, swept over them before finally settling on Alia.

Alia felt a wave of apprehension wash over her. This creature of legend, its motives shrouded in mystery, had intervened and saved them. But was it friend or foe?

In a voice that rumbled like thunder, the Sky Stalker spoke. Not words, but a series of images and emotions projected directly into Alia's mind. It spoke of a balance disrupted, of a creeping darkness that threatened the world. It spoke of its duty as guardian, a protector against those who sought to upset the natural order.

Alia, overwhelmed by the telepathic communication, struggled to comprehend the Sky Stalker's message. But one thing was clear - it wasn't an enemy. It shared a similar goal of defending the world from the encroaching darkness.

As Alia managed to piece together the fragmented emotions and images, she projected a sense of gratitude and a hesitant query back at the creature. "We seek a way to seal the darkness," she thought, her mind feeling raw from the exertion. "Can you guide us?"

The Sky Stalker studied her for a moment, its gaze penetrating. Then, with a single, powerful flap of its wings, it soared into the sky, its luminous body cutting through the darkness.

Without hesitation, Alia turned to the group. "It's leading the way," she declared, her voice filled with a mixture of relief and apprehension. "We follow."

Hope rekindled in the weary faces of the villagers. The Sky Stalker, a creature of immense power, was their guide now. With renewed determination, they followed its luminous trail, venturing deeper into the desolate heart of the Blighted Lands.

The path grew steeper, the air colder. The darkness pressed down upon them, a thick, suffocating blanket that seemed to sap their energy with every step. The whispers remained absent, offering no guidance in this corrupted land.

Days turned into a blur of treacherous climbs, howling winds, and biting cold. The Sky Stalker, a silent beacon above them, remained their only hope. Finally, after what felt like an eternity, they reached the base of the jagged peak that dominated the Blighted Lands.

A gaping maw split the mountainside, pulsating with a malevolent red light. The source of the corruption, the heart of the Blighted Lands – they had arrived.

But as they approached the fissure, the ground trembled beneath their feet. A guttural roar echoed from the depths of the mountain, followed by the shriek of tearing rock and the rumble of falling debris. As the dust settled, a horrifying sight met their eyes.

An enormous creature, its body a grotesque amalgamation of jagged rock and pulsating flesh, emerged from the fissure. It was the embodiment of the Blighted

Lands' corruption, a monstrosity fueled by the Shadow King's lingering power.

Alia, her heart pounding in her chest, recognized it from the fragmented whispers – the Blight Guardian, a monstrous entity tasked with guarding the heart of the darkness. Their path to the artifact was now blocked by this terrifying creature.

Fear threatened to engulf Alia, but the desperate faces of the villagers behind her fueled her determination. This was not the time to falter. They had come too far to turn back now.

With a deep breath, Alia focused her mind, reaching out for any remnant of the whispers. The absence of guidance in the Blighted Lands had been unnerving, but now, standing before this monstrous guardian, she yearned for even the faintest hint of direction.

A flicker, faint but undeniable, stirred within her. An image, fleeting and fragmented, flashed in her vision – a shimmering shield, pulsating with radiant energy, lying dormant within the fissure. It was the artifact, the key to sealing away the darkness. But it was likely guarded by the Blight Guardian, a terrifying opponent that stood between them and their objective.

Sharing her vision with the group, Alia laid out their predicament. Fear etched lines on the faces of the villagers, but their resolve remained intact. Elara stepped forward, her voice surprisingly steady. "We knew there would be challenges," she said. "We faced the Shadow King, and we emerged victorious. We can overcome this too."

The blacksmith, ever the pragmatist, offered a different perspective. "Victory is one thing, facing a monstrosity like that another," he countered, gesturing towards the Blight Guardian. "We need a plan, not just courage."

Alia understood his concern. This wasn't a mindless horde of Shadowborn; this was a creature born from the very essence of the Blighted Lands. But without a plan, they were nothing more than prey.

Looking back at the villagers, Alia saw a reflection of her own fear, but also a flicker of defiance. These weren't just villagers anymore; they were guardians, bonded by their connection to the whispers and their shared experience of facing the darkness.

Taking a deep breath, Alia spoke. "We may not be able to defeat the Blight Guardian head-on," she admitted, "but we can distract it. Maybe then, we can access the fissure and retrieve the artifact."

Elara nodded, a spark of understanding glinting in her eyes. "A diversion," she said. "We can use our knowledge of the whispers to create a disturbance, draw the creature's attention away from the fissure."

Their plan wouldn't be easy, and the risks were high. But it was their only chance. With a determined look, Alia scanned the group. "We need skilled fighters to draw the creature's attention. The blacksmith and I will create the disturbance. The rest of you, find cover and stay alert."

The blacksmith, a broad grin splitting his face, hefted his axe. "Sounds like a job for us bruisers."

Alia felt a wave of gratitude wash over her. Fear remained, but it was overshadowed by a sense of unity and purpose.

They were in this together, and they would face whatever challenges awaited.

As the Sky Stalker circled overhead, casting an eerie glow on the scene, the group dispersed. The fighters, led by the blacksmith, positioned themselves strategically, their weapons glinting in the faint light. Alia, drawing on the faint whispers and Elara's knowledge of ancient herbal remedies, concocted a potent mixture of volatile concoctions.

With a shared nod, Alia and the blacksmith charged towards the Blight Guardian. They were met with a deafening roar as the creature lumbered towards them, its eyes blazing with a malevolent red light. The fight was brutal, a desperate struggle against an opponent of unimaginable strength.

But their objective wasn't victory; it was distraction. While the fighters held the Blight Guardian's attention, Alia and Elara sprinted towards the fissure. The closer they got, the stronger the pulsating red light, the corrupted energy threatening to engulf them.

Just as they reached the entrance to the fissure, the air shimmered, and a transparent shield materialized before them. It pulsed with a vibrant blue light, resonating with the whispers in Alia's mind. This was the artifact – the Guardian's Shield.

With trembling hands, Alia reached out, feeling a surge of energy flow through her arm. The shield detached from the fissure with a gentle hum, the pulsating red light within the fissure diminishing ever so slightly.

But their victory was short-lived. A guttural roar announced the Blight Guardian's return. The fighters, battered but resolute, were no longer a match for the enraged creature.

Elara grabbed Alia's arm, her face etched with urgency. "We have what we came for," she said. "We need to go!"

As the Blight Guardian charged towards them, Alia looked back at the fissure, a final flicker of red light emanating from its depths. The artifact was theirs, but the darkness within wasn't fully vanquished.

With a heavy heart, Alia turned and fled with Elara, the Sky Stalker diving down to shield them from the Blight Guardian's attacks. They sprinted back towards the path they had climbed, the monstrous roar of the..Blight Guardian echoing behind them. The ground trembled with each of its earth-shattering strides, and the chilling wind whipped at their faces, carrying with it the reeking stench of decay and corruption.

Alia pushed her body to its limits, adrenaline fueling her escape. She clutched the Guardian's Shield, its blue energy pulsing with an almost comforting warmth in her hand. It was a symbol of hope, a fragile barrier against the encroaching darkness.

As they reached the treacherous path leading down the mountain, the Sky Stalker let out a deafening screech, momentarily distracting the Blight Guardian. This brief respite allowed them to descend a few precarious steps before the creature's monstrous form loomed above them again.

Elara, her breathing ragged but her eyes resolute, glanced back at the Blight Guardian. "We can't outrun it forever," she rasped. "We need to find a way to use the artifact."

Alia nodded, her mind racing. She focused on the pulsating energy within the shield, searching for any clues on how to activate its power. But the whispers were weak here, distorted by the lingering corruption.

Suddenly, a searing pain shot through her hand, tearing a gasp from her lips. The shield, pulsing with a brilliant white light, began to emit a high-pitched whine that drilled into her skull. Instinctively, she directed the shield towards the Blight Guardian.

A blinding beam of pure white light erupted from the artifact, engulfing the monstrosity in its radiant glow. The Blight Guardian recoiled with a deafening shriek, the corrupt energy emanating from its body flickering and fading.

A surge of hope washed over Alia. The shield worked! But the light began to dim, its power waning rapidly. Alia realized this was a temporary solution, a desperate measure to buy them time.

They continued their descent, the Blight Guardian hot on their heels. The creature, blinded by the shield's light, stumbled and roared in frustration. But the beam was weakening, its brilliance fading with every passing second.

Just as the light sputtered and died, plunging them back into darkness, they reached the base of the mountain. The Blight Guardian, its rage renewed, lumbered towards them.

Alia, her heart pounding in her chest, scanned their surroundings. There was nowhere to run. They were trapped between a monstrous guardian and a treacherous drop into the abyss below.

But then, as if guided by an unseen hand, Elara pointed towards a barely visible tunnel hidden in the shadows at the foot of the mountain. "There!" she cried, her voice hoarse with exertion. "A passage!"

Without hesitation, Alia sprinted towards the tunnel, the villagers close behind. Just as they reached the entrance, the Blight Guardian's massive form filled the narrow opening. It let out a frustrated roar, its claws scraping against the rock as it tried to force its way through.

But the tunnel was too small for its colossal body. Stuck and enraged, the Blight Guardian roared in frustration, its bellows echoing through the passage.

Alia, taking a deep breath, turned to her companions. "It won't fit through," she said, a glimmer of relief in her voice. "We need to go further inside, find another way out."

The tunnel was dark and damp, the air stale and heavy. They stumbled forward, relying on the faint bioluminescence of certain fungi clinging to the walls for light. The whispers, though faint, seemed to guide them deeper into the heart of the mountain.

As they ventured deeper, the tunnel opened into a vast cavern. The air shimmered with an otherworldly blue light emanating from a colossal crystal that dominated the center of the chamber.

Alia gasped. This place resonated with a powerful energy, a counterpoint to the darkness they had encountered in the Blighted Lands. It felt... ancient, a source of immense power.

Focusing her mind, she reached out with the whispers. Images flooded her vision – a forgotten race, guardians of nature who harnessed the crystal's energy to maintain balance, a detailed blueprint of the artifact clutched in her hand.

The whispers revealed this cavern to be a sanctuary, a hidden haven built by those who had fought the darkness eons ago. The Guardian's Shield, they revealed, was only one part of a larger mechanism – a device that could seal the darkness away for good.

With renewed hope, Alia turned to her companions, her heart pounding with excitement. They weren't just leaving with a weapon; they had stumbled upon a forgotten secret, a way to permanently mend the broken balance. But using this ancient device wouldn't be easy. The whispers revealed a complex ritual, requiring the combined focus of all their remaining energy.

Exhausted but determined, the group gathered around the crystal, the Guardian's Shield ...pulsating in Alia's hand. The whispers, clear and strong within the cavern, guided them through the intricate ritual. They learned that the crystal, fueled by their combined connection to nature, would amplify the shield's power, creating an energy surge capable of severing the Blighted Lands' link to the source of darkness.

Elara, her voice filled with ancient wisdom gleaned from the whispers, began the chant. The villagers, their faces etched with determination, joined in, their voices echoing through the cavern. Alia, acting as the conduit, channeled the energy from the crystal into the shield.

The cavern pulsed with vibrant blue light as the ritual reached its climax. The Guardian's Shield, no longer a passive barrier, hummed with newfound power. With a collective shout, fueled by exhaustion and hope, they unleashed the surge of energy.

A blinding light erupted from the shield, engulfing the cavern and searing through the tunnel leading back to the Blighted Lands. They squeezed their eyes shut, bracing for the impact. The very mountain trembled around them as a thunderous roar echoed from the depths.

When they finally opened their eyes, the cavern was bathed in a soft, blue light emanating from the crystal. The whispers, vibrant and clear, filled their minds with a sense of peace and harmony. Relief washed over Alia, a wave of exhaustion threatening to pull her under.

They had done it. They had severed the source of darkness, severing the Blighted Lands' corruption. But with victory came the realization of the sacrifices made. Many of the villagers wouldn't return; they had fallen prey to the Shadowborn or the treacherous journey.

As the group emerged from the tunnel, blinking in the harsh sunlight, they were greeted by a sight that filled them with awe. The desolate wasteland that had been the Blighted Lands was transforming. The barren ground was slowly being replaced by patches of green, a faint scent of life replacing the stench of decay.

The Sky Stalker, circling overhead, let out a triumphant screech before soaring off into the distance. Its duty fulfilled, it had vanished as mysteriously as it had appeared.

With heavy hearts but renewed hope, the remaining villagers began the long journey back to Eldoria. They carried with them not only the Guardian's Shield, a symbol of their victory, but also the knowledge gleaned from the ancient sanctuary. They were no longer just villagers; they were guardians, bonded by their connection to nature and forever marked by their encounter with the darkness.

The whispers, now clear and strong, guided them as they walked. The world was healing, the balance restored. But they knew their journey wasn't over. The darkness, though weakened, wouldn't be completely vanquished. There would be other threats, other challenges. But now, they were prepared.

As Alia looked back at the Blighted Lands, slowly giving way to life, she knew this was just the beginning. Their story, whispered on the wind, would serve as a reminder: even in the darkest of times, when nature calls, there will always be those who answer.

About the Author

Mrigendra Bharti, born on June 29, 2004, in South Delhi, India, is a multifaceted individual recognized as the owner of Mrigendra Bharti Group InfoTech India Co. Pvt Ltd. Beyond his entrepreneurial endeavors, he is a distinguished music producer, director, and a budding writer.

Embarking on his professional journey at a young age, Mrigendra Bharti's visionary leadership has led to the establishment of several successful ventures, including Croma Music Series Entertainment, Sellbrochure, Fauget Innovative, and more.

What sets Mrigendra apart is his early initiation into the world of business. His foray into the unknown realms of entrepreneurship began during his 10th-grade years, where he delved into the music industry. This initial venture laid the foundation for subsequent achievements, showcasing his dedication and resilience.

Having honed his skills in music, Mrigendra Bharti not only demonstrated significant growth in his craft but also expanded his professional network. His passion extends beyond music, encompassing app and website development, as well as graphic design.

Fueled by his creative aspirations, Mrigendra established the Mrigendra Bharti Group, a company specializing in website and app development. Currently, he collaborates with a dedicated team, collectively working on ambitious projects that promise innovation and excellence.

Mrigendra's journey serves as an inspiration, particularly for today's students, highlighting the potential of youthful determination and the ability to transform innovative ideas into successful businesses. As he continues to make strides in various domains, Mrigendra Bharti remains a dynamic force, contributing vibrancy to the realms of business, music, and technology.

Read more at https://www.imwriter-mrigendra.rf.gd.